MARTA RIQUELME
SOUTH AMERICAN ROMANCES

W.H. HUDSON

British Library Cataloguing-in-Publication Data
A catalogue record for this book is available from the
British Library

William Henry Hudson

William Henry Hudson was born on 4 August 1841 in a borough of Quilmes (now Florecio Varela) in Greater Buenos Aires, Argentina. His parents, Daniel and Catherine Hudson, were American settlers of English and Irish origin. His father was a sheep farmer on a small farm in Argentina, but was sadly unsuccessful. He then turned to potato growing for a paltry existence and this led the family to near financial ruin.

Hudson spent his childhood exploring the local flora and fauna and observing the natural and human drama, on what was a lawless frontier at that time. At around fourteen or fifteen, Hudson became seriously ill with a bout of typhus, soon followed by rheumatic fever. These illnesses permanently affected his health and caused him to become more studious and contemplative. His parents obtained many books for him and his siblings to read and he occasionally had some formal education from a visiting school teacher. Charles Darwin's (1809-1882) *The Origin of Species* (1859), in particular, made a lasting impression on him.

Little is known about Hudson in the period following his parents' death. He became a wanderer, occasionally publishing his ornithological work in the *Proceedings of the Zoological Society*. He initially wrote in an English that was interlaced with Spanish idioms. He appears to have particularly loved Patagonia. Hudson immigrated to London, England in 1869, where he eventually became a British subject in 1900. In 1876 he married a much older woman and they lived precariously on the money earned from two boarding houses that she owned. She eventually inherited a house in Bayswater, London and the couple moved there.

Hudson produced a series of ornithological studies throughout his life, including *Argentine Ornithology* (1888-1899) and *British Birds* (1895). These books on ornithological studies attracted the attention of the statesman, Sir Edward Grey (1862-1933), who got Hudson a state pension in 1901. Hudson later achieved fame with his books on the English countryside, such as *Hampshire Day* (1903), *Afoot in England* (1909), and *A Shepherd's Life* (1910), which helped foster the back to nature movement of the 1920s and 1930s. His most famous fictional novel was *Green Mansions* (1904) which was an exotic romance about a traveller in the Guyana Jungle in Venezuela and his encounter with a mysterious forest girl who is half human and half bird. This romance and some of Hudson's other romances attracted the friendship of other fiction writers, such as Joseph Conrad (1857-

1924), Ford Madox Ford (1873-1939) and George Gissing (1857-1903). Hudson's most popular non-fiction novel was *Far Away and Long Ago* (1918) which recalls his childhood in Argentina. Some of his other titles include *Birds and Man* (1901), *A Little Lost Boy* (1905), *Tales of the Pampas* (1916), *Ralph Herne* (1923), and *Mary's Little Lamb* (1929).

Away from his literary work, Hudson was a founding member of the Royal Society for the Protection of Birds. Towards the end of his life he moved to Worthing, Sussex, England. He died on 18 August 1922 and is buried at Broadwater and Worthing Cemetery in Worthing where his epitaph refers to his love of birds and green places. Even after his death, Hudson had a huge legacy. In Argentina where he is known as Guillermo Enrique Hudson, his work is considered to belong to the national literature. Ernest Hemingway (1899-1961) also famously refers to Hudson's early book *The Purple Land* (1885) in his novel *The Sun Also Rises* (1926) and again to Hudson's *Far Away and Long Ago* in his posthumous novel, *The Garden of Eden* (1986). Hudson has also had two South American bird species named after him as well as a town in Berazategui Partidd and several other public places and institutions.

CONTENTS

CHAPTER

MARTA RIQUELME
(*From the Sepulvida MSS.*)

CHAPTER I

F AR away from the paths of those who wander to and
fro on the earth, sleeps Jujuy in the heart of this
continent. It is the remotest of our provinces, and
divided from the countries of the Pacific by the giant
range of the Cordillera ; a region of mountains and forest,
torrid heats and great storms ; and although in itself a
country half as large as the Spanish peninsula, it possesses,
as its only means of communication with the outside
world, a few insignificant roads which are scarcely more
than mule-paths.

The people of this region have few wants ; they aspire
not after progress, and have never changed their ancient
manner of life. The Spanish were long in conquering
them ; and now, after three centuries of Christian
dominion, they still speak the Quichua, and subsist in a
great measure on patay, a sweet paste made from the pod
of the wild algarroba tree ; while they still retain as a
beast of burden the llama, a gift of their old masters the
Peruvian Incas.

This much is common knowledge, but of the peculiar
character of the country, or of the nature of the things

1

which happen within its borders, nothing is known to those without ; Jujuy being to them only a country lying over against the Andes, far removed from and unaffected by the progress of the world. It has pleased Providence to give me a more intimate knowledge, and this has been a sore affliction and great burden now for many years. But I have not taken up my pen to complain that all the years of my life are consumed in a region where the great spiritual enemy of mankind is still permitted to challenge the supremacy of our Master, waging an equal war against his followers : my sole object is to warn, perhaps also to comfort, others who will be my successors in this place and who will come to the church of Yala ignorant of the means which will be used for the destruction of their souls. And if I set down anything in this narrative which might be injurious to our holy religion, owing to the darkness of our understanding and the little faith that is in us, I pray that the sin I now ignorantly commit may be forgiven me, and that this manuscript may perish miraculously unread by any person.

I was educated for the priesthood in the city of Cordova, that famous seminary of learning and religion ; and in 1838, being then in my twenty-seventh year, I was appointed priest to a small settlement in the distant province of which I have spoken. The habit of obedience, early instilled in me by my Jesuit masters, enabled me to accept this command unmurmuringly, and even with an outward show of cheerfulness. Nevertheless it filled me with grief, although I might have suspected that some such hard fate had been designed for me, since I had been made to study the Quichua language, which is now only spoken in the Andean provinces. With secret bitter repinings I tore myself from all that made life pleasant and desirable—the society of innumerable friends, the libraries, the beautiful church where I had worshipped, and that renowned University which has shed on the troubled annals of our unhappy country whatever lustre of learning and poetry they possess.

My first impressions of Jujuy did not serve to raise my spirits. After a trying journey of four weeks' duration— the roads being difficult and the country greatly disturbed at the time—I reached the capital of the province, also called Jujuy, a town of about two thousand inhabitants. Thence I journeyed to my destination, a settlement called Yala, situated on the north-western border of the province, where the river Yala takes its rise, at the foot of that range of mountains which, branching eastwards from the Andes, divides Jujuy from Bolivia. I was wholly unprepared for the character of the place I had come to live in. Yala was a scattered village of about ninety souls—ignorant, apathetic people, chiefly Indians. To my unaccustomed sight the country appeared a rude, desolate chaos of rocks and gigantic mountains, compared with which the famous sierras of Cordova sunk into mere hillocks, and of vast gloomy forests, whose death-like stillness was broken only by the savage screams of some strange fowl, or by the hoarse thunders of a distant waterfall.

As soon as I had made myself known to the people of the village, I set myself to acquire a knowledge of the

surrounding country ; but before long I began to despair
of ever finding the limits of my parish in any direction.
The country was wild, being only tenanted by a few
widely-separated families, and like all deserts it was
distasteful to me in an eminent degree ; but as I would
frequently be called upon to perform long journeys, I
resolved to learn as much as possible of its geography.
Always striving to overcome my own inclinations, which
made a studious, sedentary life most congenial, I aimed at
being very active ; and having procured a good mule I
began taking long rides every day, without a guide and
with only a pocket compass to prevent me from losing
myself. I could never altogether overcome my natural
aversion to silent deserts, and in my long rides I avoided
the thick forest and deep valleys, keeping as much as
possible to the open plain.

One day having ridden about twelve or fourteen miles
from Yala, I discovered a tree of noble proportions growing
by itself in the open, and feeling much oppressed by the
heat I alighted from my mule and stretched myself on the
ground under the grateful shade. There was a continuous
murmur of lecheguanas—a small honey wasp—in the
foliage above me, for the tree was in flower, and this
soothing sound soon brought that restful feeling to my
mind which insensibly leads to slumber. I was, however,
still far from sleep, but reclining with eyes half closed,
thinking of nothing, when suddenly, from the depths of
the dense leafage above me, rang forth a shriek, the most
terrible it has ever fallen to the lot of any human being to
hear. In sound it was a human cry, yet expressing a

degree of agony and despair surpassing the power of any human soul to feel, and my impression was that it could only have been uttered by some tortured spirit allowed to wander for a season on the earth. Shriek after shriek, each more powerful and terrible to hear than the last, succeeded, and I sprang to my feet, the hair standing erect on my head, a profuse sweat of terror breaking out all over me. The cause of all these maddening sounds remained invisible to my eyes; and finally running to my mule, I climbed hastily on to its back and never ceased flogging the poor beast all the way back to Yala.

On reaching my house I sent for one Osuna, a man of substance, able to converse in Spanish, and much respected in the village. In the evening he came to see me, and I then gave an account of the extraordinary experience I had encountered that day.

" Do not distress yourself, Father—you have only heard the Kakué," he replied. I then learnt from him that the Kakué is a fowl frequenting the most gloomy and sequestered forests and known to everyone in the country for its terrible voice. Kakué, he also informed me, was the ancient name of the country, but the word was misspelt Jujuy by the early explorers, and this corrupted name was eventually retained. All this, which I now heard for the first time, is historical; but when he proceeded to inform me that the Kakué is a metamorphosed human being, that women and sometimes men, whose lives have been darkened with great suffering and calamities, are changed by compassionate spirits into the lugubrious birds, I asked him somewhat contemptuously whether he, an enlightened man, believed a thing so absurd.

" There is not in all Jujuy," he replied, " a person who disbelieves it."

" That is a mere assertion," cried I, " but it shows which way your mind inclines. No doubt the superstition concerning the Kakué is very ancient, and has come down to us together with the Quichua language from the aborigines. Transformations of men into animals are common in all the primitive religions of South America. Thus, the Guarines relate that flying from a conflagration caused by the descent of the sun to the earth many people cast themselves into the river Paraguay, and were incontinently changed into capybaras and caymans ; while others who took refuge in trees were blackened and scorched by the heat and became monkeys. But to go no further than the traditions of the Incas who once ruled over this region, it is related that after the first creation the entire human family, inhabiting the slopes of the Andes, were changed into crickets by a demon at enmity with man's first creator. Throughout the continent these ancient beliefs are at present either dead or dying out ; and if the Kakué legend still maintains its hold on the vulgar here it is owing to the isolated position of the country, hemmed in by vast mountains and having no intercourse with neighbouring states."

Perceiving that my arguments had entirely failed to produce any effect I began to lose my temper, and demanded whether he, a Christian, dared to profess belief in a fable born of the corrupt imagination of the heathen ?

MARTA RIQUELME

He shrugged his shoulders and replied, " I have only stated what we, in Jujuy, know to be a fact. What is, is ; and if you talk until to-morrow you cannot make it different, although you may prove yourself a very learned person."

His answer produced a strange effect on me. For the first time in my life I experienced the sensation of anger in all its power. Rising to my feet I paced the floor excitedly, and using many gestures, smiting the table with my hands and shaking my clenched fist close to his face in a threatening manner, and with a violence of language unbecoming to a follower of Christ, I denounced the degrading ignorance and heathenish condition of mind of the people I had come to live with ; and more particularly of the person before me, who had some pretensions to education and should have been free from the gross delusions of the vulgar. While addressing him in this tone he sat smoking a cigarette, blowing rings from his lips, and placidly watching them rise towards the ceiling, and with his studied supercilious indifference aggravated my rage to such a degree that I could scarcely restrain myself from flying at his throat or striking him to the earth with one of the cane-bottomed chairs in the room.

As soon as he left me, however, I was overwhelmed with remorse at having behaved in a manner so unseemly. I spent the night in penitent tears and prayer, and resolved in future to keep a strict watch over myself, now that the secret enemy of my soul had revealed itself to me. Nor did I make this resolution a moment too soon. I had hitherto

7

regarded myself as a person of a somewhat mild and placid disposition; the sudden change to new influences, and, perhaps also, the secret disgust I felt at my lot, had quickly developed my true character, which now became impatient to a degree and prone to sudden violent outbursts of passion during which I had little control over my tongue. The perpetual watch over myself and struggle against my evil nature which had now become necessary was the cause of but half my trouble. I discovered that my parishioners, with scarcely an exception, possessed that dull apathetic temper of mind concerning spiritual things, which has so greatly exasperated me in the man Osuna, and which obstructed all my efforts to benefit them. These people, or rather their ancestors centuries ago, had accepted Christianity, but it had never properly filtered down into their hearts. It was on the surface still; and if their half-heathen minds were deeply stirred it was not by the story of the Passion of our Lord, but by some superstitious belief inherited from their progenitors. During all the years I have spent in Yala I never said a Mass, never preached a sermon, never attempted to speak of the consolations of faith, without having the thought thrust on to me that my words were useless, that I was watering the rock where no seed could germinate, and wasting my life in vain efforts to impart religion to souls that were proof against it. Often have I been reminded of our holy and learned Father Guevara's words, when he complains of the difficulties encountered by the earlier Jesuit missionaries. He relates how one endeavoured to impress the Chiriguanos with the danger they incurred by refusing baptism, picturing to them their future condition when they would be condemned to everlasting fire. To which they only replied that they were not disturbed by what he told them, but were, on the contrary, greatly pleased to hear that the flames of the future would be unquenchable, for that would save them infinite trouble, and if they found the fire too hot they would remove themselves to a proper distance from it. So hard it was for their heathen intellects to comprehend the solemn doctrines of our faith !

CHAPTER II

MY knowledge of the Quichua language, acquired solely by the study of the vocabularies, was at first of little advantage to me. I found myself unable to converse on familiar topics with the people of Yala; and this was a great difficulty in my way, and a cause of distress for more reasons than one. I was unprovided with books, or other means of profit and recreation, and therefore eagerly sought out the few people in the place able to converse in Spanish, for I have always been fond of social intercourse. There were only four: one very old man, who died shortly after my arrival; another was Osuna, a man for whom I had conceived an unconquerable aversion; the other two were women, the widow Riquelme and her daughter. About this girl I must speak at some length, since it is with her fortunes that this narrative is chiefly concerned. The widow Riquelme was poor, having only a house in Yala, but with a garden sufficiently large to grow a plentiful provision of fruit and vegetables, and to feed a few goats, so that these women had enough to live on, without ostentation, from their plot of ground. They were of pure Spanish blood; the mother was prematurely old and faded; Marta, who was a little over fifteen when I arrived at Yala, was the loveliest being I had ever beheld; though in this matter my opinion may be biased, for I only saw her side by side with the dark-skinned coarse-haired Indian women, and compared with their faces of ignoble type Marta's was like that of an angel. Her features were regular; her skin white, but with that pale darkness in it seen in some whose families have lived for generations in tropical countries. Her eyes, shaded by long lashes, were of that violet tint seen sometimes in people of Spanish blood—eyes which appear black until looked at closely. Her hair was however the crown of her beauty and chief glory, for it was of great length and a dark shining gold colour—a thing wonderful to see!

The society of these two women, who were full of sympathy and sweetness, promised to be a great boon to me, and I was often with them; but very soon I discovered that, on the contrary, it was only about to add a fresh bitterness to my existence. The Christian affection I felt for this beautiful child insensibly degenerated into a mundane passion of such overmastering strength that all my efforts to pluck it out of my heart proved ineffectual. I cannot describe my unhappy condition during the long months when I vainly wrestled with this sinful emotion, and when I often thought in the bitterness of my heart that my God had forsaken me. The fear that the time would come when my feelings would betray themselves increased on me until at length, to avoid so great an evil, I was compelled to cease visiting the only house in Yala where it was a pleasure for me to enter. What had I done to be thus cruelly persecuted by Satan? was the constant cry of my soul. Now I know that this temptation was only a part of that long and desperate struggle in which the servants of the prince of the power of the air had engaged to overthrow me.

Not for five years did this conflict with myself cease to be a constant danger—a period which seemed to my mind not less than half a century. Nevertheless, knowing that idleness is the parent of evil, I was incessantly occupied ; for when there was nothing to call me abroad, I laboured with my pen at home, filling in this way many volumes, which in the end may serve to throw some light on the great historical question of the Incas' Cis-Andine dominion, and its effect on the conquered nations.

When Marta was twenty years old it became known in Yala that she had promised her hand in marriage to one Cosme Luna, and of this person a few words must be said. Like many young men, possessing no property or occupation, and having no disposition to work, he was a confirmed gambler, spending all his time going about from town to town to attend horse-races and cock-fights. I had for a long time regarded him as an abominable pest in Yala, a wretch possessing a hundred vices under a pleasing exterior, and not one redeeming virtue, and it was therefore with the deepest pain that I heard of his success with Marta. The widow, who was naturally disappointed at her daughter's choice, came to me with tears and complaints begging me to assist her in persuading her beloved child to break off an engagement which promised only to make her unhappy for life. But with that secret feeling in my heart, ever-striving to drag me down to my ruin, I dared not help her, albeit, I would gladly have given my right hand to save Marta from the calamity of marrying such a man.

The tempest which these tidings had raised in my heart never abated while the preparations for the marriage were going on. I was forced now to abandon my work, for I was incapable of thought; nor did all my religious exercises avail to banish for one moment the strange, sullen rage which had taken complete possession of me. Night after night I would rise from my bed and pace the floor of my room for hours, vainly trying to shut out the promptings of some fiend perpetually urging me to take some desperate course against this young man. A thousand schemes for his destruction suggested themselves to my mind, and when I had resolutely dismissed them all and prayed that my sinful temper might be forgiven, I would rise from my knees still cursing him a thousand times more than ever.

In the meantime, Marta herself saw nothing wrong in Cosme, for love had blinded her. He was young, good looking, could play on the guitar and sing, and was master of that easy, playful tone in conversation which is always pleasing to women. Moreover, he dressed well and was generous with his money, with which he was apparently well provided.

In due time they were married, and Cosme, having no house of his own, came to live with his mother-in-law in Yala. Then, at length, what I had foreseen also happened. He ran out of money, and his new relations had nothing he could lay his hands on to sell. He was too proud to gamble for coppers, and the poor people of Yala

13

had no silver to risk ; he could not or would not work, and the vacant life he was living began to grow wearisome. Once more he took to his old courses, and it soon grew to be a common thing for him to be absent from home for a month or six weeks at a time. Marta looked unhappy, but would not complain or listen to a word against Cosme ; for whenever he returned to Yala then his wife's great beauty was like a new thing to him, bringing him to her feet, and making him again for a brief season her devoted lover and slave.

She at length became a mother. For her sake I was glad ; for now with her infant boy to occupy her mind, Cosme's neglect would seem more endurable. He was away when the child was born ; he had gone, it was reported, into Catamarca, and for three months nothing was heard of him. This was a season of political troubles, and men being required to recruit the forces, all persons found wandering about the country not engaged in any lawful occupation, were taken for military service. And this had happened to Cosme. A letter from him reached Marta at last, informing her that he had been carried away to San Luis, and asking her to send him two hundred pesos, as with that amount he would be able to purchase his release. But it was impossible for her to raise the money : nor could she leave Yala to go to him, for her mother's strength was now rapidly failing, and Marta could not abandon her to the care of strangers. All this she was obliged to tell Cosme in the letter she wrote to him, and which perhaps never reached his hands, for no reply to it ever came.

MARTA RIQUELME

At length, the widow Riquelme died; then Marta sold the house and garden and all she possessed, and taking her child with her, went out to seek her husband. Travelling first to the town of Jujuy, she there, with other women, attached herself to a convoy about to start on a journey to the southern provinces. Several months went by, and then came the disastrous tidings to Yala that the convoy had been surprised by Indians in a lonely place and all the people slain.

I will not here dwell on the anguish of mind I endured on learning Marta's sad end; for I tried hard to believe that her troubled life was indeed over, although I was often assured by my neighbours that the Indians invariably spare the women and children.

Every blow dealt by a cruel destiny against this most unhappy woman had pierced my heart; and during the years that followed, and when the villagers had long ceased to speak of her, often in the dead of the night I rose and sought the house where she had lived, and walking under the trees in the garden where I had so often held intercourse with her, indulged a grief which time seemed powerless to mitigate.

CHAPTER III

MARTA was not dead; but what happened to her after her departure from Yala was this: When the convoy with which she journeyed was attacked the men only were slain, while the women and children were carried away into captivity. When the victors divided the spoil among themselves, the child, which even in that long painful journey into the desert, with the prospect of a life of cruel slavery before her, had been a comfort to Marta, was taken forcibly from her arms to be conveyed to some distant place, and from that moment she utterly lost sight of it. She was herself bought by an Indian able to pay for a pretty white captive, and who presently made her his wife. She, a Christian, the wife of a man loved only too well, could not endure this horrible fate which had overtaken her. She was also mad with grief at the loss of her child, and stealing out one dark stormy night she fled from the Indian settlement. For several days and nights she wandered about the desert, suffering every hardship and in constant fear of jaguars, and was at length found by the savages in a half-starved condition and unable longer to fly from them. Her owner, when she was restored to him, had no mercy on her: he bound her to a tree growing beside his hovel, and there every day he cruelly scourged her naked flesh to satisfy his barbarous resentment, until she was ready to perish with excessive suffering. He also cut off her hair, and braiding it into a belt wore it always round his waist,—a golden trophy which doubtless won him great honour and distinction amongst his fellow savages. When he had by these means utterly broken her spirit and reduced her to the last condition of weakness, he released her from the tree, but at the same time fastened a log of wood to her ankle, so that only with great labour and drawing herself along with the aid of her hands, could she perform the daily tasks her master imposed on her. Only after a whole year of captivity, and when she had given birth to a child, was the punishment over and her foot released from the log. The natural affection which she felt for this child of a father so cruel was now poor Marta's only comfort. In this hard servitude five years of her miserable existence were consumed ; and only those who know the stern, sullen, pitiless character of the Indian can imagine what this period was for Marta, without sympathy from her fellow-creatures, with no hope and no pleasure beyond the pleasure of loving and caressing her own infant savages. Of these she was now the mother of three.

When her youngest was not many months old Marta had one day wandered some distance in search of sticks for firewood, when a woman, one of her fellow-captives from Jujuy, came running to her, for she had been watching for an opportunity of speaking with Marta. It happened that this woman had succeeded in persuading her Indian husband to take her back to her home in the

BB

Christian country, and she had at the same time won his consent to take Marta with them, having conceived a great affection for her. The prospect of escape filled poor Marta's heart with joy, but when she was told that her children could on no account be taken, then a cruel struggle commenced in her breast. Bitterly she pleaded for permission to take her babes, and at last overcome by her importunity her fellow-captive consented to her taking the youngest of the three ; though this concession was made very reluctantly.

In a short time the day appointed for the flight arrived and Marta carrying her infant met her friends in the wood. They were quickly mounted, and the journey began which was to last for many days, and during which they were to suffer much from hunger, thirst and fatigue. One dark night as they journeyed through a hilly and wooded country, Marta being overcome with fatigue so that she could scarcely keep her seat, the Indian, with affected kindness, relieved her of the child she always carried in her arms. An hour passed, and then pressing forward to his side and asking for her child she was told that it had been dropped into a deep, swift stream over which they had swam their horses some time before. Of what happened after that she was unable to give any very clear account. She only dimly remembered that through many days of scorching heat and many nights of weary travel she was always piteously pleading for her lost child—always seeming to hear it crying to her to save it from destruction. The long journey ended at last. She was left by the other at the first Christian settlement they reached, after which, travelling slowly from village to village, she made her way to Yala. Her old neighbours and friends did not know her at first, but when they were at length convinced that it was indeed Marta Riquelme that stood before them she was welcomed like one returned from the grave. I heard of her arrival, and hastening forth to greet her found her seated before a neighbour's house already surrounded by half the people of the village.

Was this woman indeed Marta, once the pride of Yala! It was hard to believe it, so darkened with the burning suns and winds of years was her face, once so fair; so wasted and furrowed with grief and the many hardships she had undergone! Her figure, worn almost to a skeleton, was clothed with ragged garments, while her head, bowed down with sorrow and despair, was divested of that golden crown which had been her chief ornament. Seeing me arrive she cast herself on her knees before me and taking my hands in hers covered it with tears and kisses. The grief I felt at the sight of her forlorn condition mingled with joy for her deliverance from death and captivity overcame me; I was shaken like a reed in the wind, and covering my face with my robe I sobbed aloud in the presence of all the people.

CHAPTER IV

EVERYTHING that charity could dictate was done to alleviate her misery. A merciful woman of Yala received her into her house and provided her with decent garments. But for a time nothing served to raise her desponding spirits; she still grieved for her lost babe, and seemed ever in fancy listening to its piteous cries for help. When assured that Cosme would return in due time, that alone gave her comfort. She believed what they told her, for it agreed with her wish, and by degrees the effects of her terrible experience began to wear off, giving place to a feeling of feverish impatience, with which she looked forward to her husband's return. With this feeling, which I did all I could to encourage, perceiving it to be the only remedy against despair, came also a new anxiety about her personal appearance. She grew careful in her dress, and made the most of her short and sunburnt hair. Beauty she could never recover; but she possessed good features which could not be altered; her eyes also retained their violet colour, and hope brought back to her something of the vanished expression of other years.

At length, when she had been with us over a year, one day there came a report that Cosme had arrived, that he had been seen in Yala, and had alighted at Andrada's door—the store in the main road. She heard it and rose up with a great cry of joy. He had come to her at last— he would comfort her! She could not wait for his arrival: what wonder! Hurrying forth she flew like the wind through the village, and in a few moments stood on Andrada's threshold, panting from her race, her cheeks glowing, all the hope and life and fire of her girlhood rushing back to her heart. There she beheld Cosme, changed but little, surrounded by his old companions, listening in silence and with a dismayed countenance to the story of Marta's sufferings in the great desert, of her escape and return to Yala, where she had been received like one come back from the sepulchre. Presently they caught sight of her standing there. "Here is Marta herself arrived in good time," they cried. "Behold your wife!"

He shook himself from them with a strange laugh. "What, that woman my wife—Marta Riquelme!" he replied. "No, no, my friends, be not deceived; Marta perished long ago in the desert, where I have been to seek for her. Of her death I have no doubt; let me pass."

He pushed by her, left her standing there motionless as a statue, unable to utter a word, and was quickly on his horse riding away from Yala.

Then suddenly she recovered possession of her faculties, and with a cry of anguish hurried after him, imploring him to return to her; but finding that he would not listen to her she was overcome with despair and fell upon the earth insensible. She was taken up by the people who had followed her out and carried back into the house. Unhappily she was not dead, and when she recovered consciousness it was pitiful to hear the excuses she invented for the remorseless wretch who had abandoned her. She was altered, she said, greatly altered—it was not strange that Cosme had refused to believe that she could be the Marta of six years ago! In her heart she knew that nobody was deceived : to all Yala it was patent that she had been deserted. She could not endure it, and when she met people in the street she lowered her eyes and passed on, pretending not to see them. Most of her time was spent indoors, and there she would sit for hours without speaking or stirring, her cheeks resting on her hands, her eyes fixed on vacancy. My heart bled for her ; morning and evening I remembered her in my prayers ; by every argument I sought to cheer her drooping spirit, even telling her that the beauty and freshness of her youth would return to her in time, and that her husband would repent and come back to her.

These efforts were fruitless. Before many days she disappeared from Yala, and though diligent search was made in the adjacent mountains she could not be found. Knowing how empty and desolate her life had been, deprived of every object of affection, I formed the opinion that she had gone back to the desert to seek the tribe where she had been a captive in the hope of once more seeing her lost children. At length, when all expectation of ever seeing her again had been abandoned, a person named Montero came to me with tidings of her. He was a poor man, a charcoal-burner, and lived with his wife and children in the forest about two hours' journey from Yala, at a distance from any other habitation. Finding Marta wandering lost in the woods he had taken her to his rancho, and she had been pleased to find this shelter, away from the people of Yala who knew her history; and it was at Marta's own request that this good man had ridden to the village to inform me of her safety. I was greatly relieved to hear all this, and thought that Marta had acted wisely in escaping from the villagers, who were always pointing her out and repeating her wonderful history. In that sequestered spot where she had taken refuge, removed from sad associations and gossiping tongues, the wounds in her heart would perhaps gradually heal and peace return to her perturbed spirit.

Before many weeks had elapsed, however, Montero's wife came to me with a very sad account of Marta. She had grown day by day more silent and solitary in her habits, spending most of her time in some secluded spot among the trees, where she would sit motionless, brooding over her memories for hours at a time. Nor was this the worst. Occasionally she would make an effort to assist in the household work, preparing the patay or maize for the supper, or going out with Montero's wife to gather firewood in the forest. But suddenly, in the middle of her task, she would drop her bundle of sticks and, casting herself on the earth, break forth into the most heart-rending cries and lamentations, loudly exclaiming that God had unjustly persecuted her, that He was a being filled with malevolence, and speaking many things against Him very dreadful to hear. Deeply distressed at these things I called for my mule and accompanied the poor woman back to her own house; but when we arrived there Marta could nowhere be found.

Most willingly would I have remained to see her, and try once more to win her back from these desponding moods, but I was compelled to return to Yala. For it happened that a fever epidemic had recently broken out and spread over the country, so that hardly a day passed without its long journey to perform and death-bed to attend. Often during those days, worn out with fatigue and want of sleep I would dismount from my mule and rest for a season against a rock or tree, wishing for death to come and release me from so sad an existence.

When I left Montero's house I charged him to send me news of Marta as soon as they should find her; but for several days I heard nothing. At length word came that they had discovered her hiding-place in the forest, but could not induce her to leave it, or even to speak to them; and they implored me to go to them, for they were greatly troubled at her state, and knew not what to do.

Once more I went out to seek her; and this was the saddest journey of all, for even the elements were charged with unusual gloom, as if to prepare my mind for some unimaginable calamity. Rain, accompanied by terrific thunder and lightning, had been falling in torrents for several days, so that the country was all but impassable: the swollen streams roared between the hills, dragging down rocks and trees, and threatening, whenever we were compelled to ford them, to carry us away to destruction. The rain had ceased, but the whole sky was covered by a dark motionless cloud, unpierced by a single ray of sunshine. The mountains, wrapped in blue vapours, loomed before us, vast and desolate ; and the trees, in that still, thick atmosphere, were like figures of trees hewn out of solid ink-black rock and set up in some shadowy subterranean region to mock its inhabitants with an imitation of the upper world.

At length we reached Montero's hut, and, followed by all the family, went to look for Marta. The place where she had concealed herself was in a dense wood half a league from the house, and the ascent to it being steep and difficult Montero was compelled to walk before, leading my mule by the bridle. At length we came to the spot where they had discovered her, and there, in the shadow of the woods, we found Marta still in the same place, seated on the trunk of a fallen tree, which was sodden with the rain and half buried under great creepers and masses of dead and rotting foliage. She was in a crouching attitude, her feet gathered under her garments, which were now torn to rags and fouled with clay ; her elbows were planted on her drawn-up knees, and her long, bony fingers thrust into her hair, which fell in tangled disorder over her face. To this pitiable condition had she been brought by great and unmerited sufferings.

Seeing her, a cry of compassion escaped my lips, and casting myself off my mule I advanced towards her. As I approached she raised her eyes to mine, and then I stood still, transfixed with amazement and horror at what I saw ; for they were no longer those soft violet orbs which had retained until recently their sweet pathetic

expression ; now they were round and wild-looking, open
to thrice their ordinary size, and filled with a lurid yellow
fire, giving them a resemblance to the eyes of some hunted
savage animal.

" Great God, she has lost her reason ! " I cried ; then
falling on my knees I disengaged the crucifix from my
neck with trembling hands, and endeavoured to hold it
up before her sight. This movement appeared to infuriate
her ; the insane, desolate eyes, from which all human
expression had vanished, became like two burning balls,
which seemed to shoot out sparks of fire ; her short hair
rose up until it stood like an immense crest on her head ;
and suddenly bringing down her skeleton-like hands she
thrust the crucifix violently from her, uttering at the
same time a succession of moans and cries that pierced
my heart with pain to hear. And presently flinging up
her arms, she burst forth into shrieks so terrible in the
depth of agony they expressed that overcome by the
sound I sank upon the earth and hid my face. The others,
who were close behind me, did likewise, for no human
soul could endure those cries, the remembrance of which,
even now after many years, causes the blood to run cold
in my veins.

" The Kakué ! The Kakué ! " exclaimed Montero,
who was close behind me.

Recalled to myself by these words I raised my eyes only
to discover that Marta was no longer before me. For
even in that moment, when those terrible cries were
ringing through my heart, waking the echoes of the
mountain solitudes, the awful change had come, and she

had looked her last with human eyes on earth and on man! In another form—that strange form of the Kakué —she had fled out of our sight for ever to hide in those gloomy woods which were henceforth to be her dwelling place. And I—most miserable of men, what had I done that all my prayers and strivings had been thus frustrated, that out of my very hands the spirit of the power of darkness had thus been permitted to wrest this unhappy soul from me!

I rose up trembling from the earth, the tears pouring unchecked down my cheeks, while the members of Montero's family gathered round me and clung to my garments. Night closed on us, black as despair and death, and with the greatest difficulty we made our way back through the woods. But I would not remain at the rancho; at the risk of my life I returned to Yala, and all through that dark solitary ride I was incessantly crying out to God to have mercy on me. Towards midnight I reached the village in safety, but the horror with which that unheard of tragedy infected me, the fears and the doubts which dared not yet shape themselves into words, remained in my breast to torture me. For days I could neither eat nor sleep. I was reduced to a skeleton and my hair began to turn white before its time. Being now incapable of performing my duties, and believing that death was approaching, I yearned once more for the city of my birth. I escaped at length from Yala, and with great difficulty reached the town of Jujuy and from thence by slow stages I journeyed back to Cordova.

CHAPTER V

"ONCE more do I behold thee, O Cordova, beautiful to my eyes as the new Jerusalem coming down from Heaven to those who have witnessed the resurrection! Here, where my life began, may I now be allowed to lie down in peace, like a tired child that falls asleep on its mother's breast."

Thus did I apostrophise my natal city, when, looking from the height above, I at last saw it before me, girdled with purple hills and bright with the sunshine, the white towers of the many churches springing out of the green mist of groves and gardens.

Nevertheless Providence ordained that in Cordova I was to find life and not death. Surrounded by old beloved friends, worshipping in the old church I knew so well, health returned to me, and I was like one who rises after a night of evil dreams and goes forth to feel the sunshine and fresh wind on his face. I told the strange story of Marta to one person only; this was Father Irala, a learned and discreet man of great piety, and one high in authority in the church at Cordova. I was astonished that he was able to listen calmly to the things I related; he spoke some consoling words, but made no attempt then or afterwards to throw any light on the mystery. In Cordova a great cloud seemed to be lifted from my mind

which left my faith unimpaired ; I was once more cheer-
ful and happy—happier than I had ever been since leaving
it. Three months went by ; then Irala told me one day
that it was time for me to return to Yala, for my health
being restored there was nothing to keep me longer from
my flock.

Oh that flock, that flock, in which for me there had been
only one precious lamb !

I was greatly disquieted ; all those nameless doubts
and fears which had left me now seemed returning ; I
begged him to spare me, to send some younger man,
ignorant of the matters I had imparted to him, to take my
place. He replied that for the very reason that I was
acquainted with those matters I was the only fit person
to go to Yala. Then in my agitation I unburdened my
heart to him. I spoke of that heathenish apathy of the
people I had struggled in vain to overcome, of the temptations I had encountered—the passion of anger and earthly
love, the impulse to commit some terrible crime. Then
had come the tragedy of Marta Riquelme and the spiritual
world had seemed to resolve itself into a chaos where
Christ was powerless to save ; in my misery and despair
my reason had almost forsaken me and I had fled from
the country. In Cordova hope had revived, my prayers
had brought an immediate response, and the Author of
salvation seemed to be near to me. Here in Cordova, I
said in conclusion, was life, but in the soul-destroying
atmosphere of Yala death eternal.

" Brother Sepulvida," he answered, " we know all your
sufferings and suffer with you : nevertheless you must

return to Yala. Though there in the enemy's country, in the midst of the fight, when hard pressed and wounded, you have perhaps doubted God's omnipotence, He calls you to the front again, where He will be with you and fight at your side. It is for you, not for us, to find the solution of those mysteries which have troubled you; and that you have already come near to the solution your own words seem to show. Remember that we are here not for our own pleasure, but to do our Master's work; that the highest reward will not be for those who sit in the cool shade, book in hand, but for the toilers in the field who are suffering the burden and heat of the day. Return to Yala and be of good heart, and in due time all things will be made clear to your understanding."

These words gave me some comfort, and meditating much on them I took my departure from Cordova, and in due time arrived at my destination.

I had, on quitting Yala, forbidden Montero and his wife to speak of the manner of Marta's disappearance, believing that it would be better for my people to remain in ignorance of such a matter; but now, when going about in the village, on my return I found that it was known to everyone. That "Marta had become a Kakué" was mentioned on all sides; yet it did not affect them with astonishment and dismay that this should be so, it was merely an event for idle women to chatter about, like Quiteria's elopement or Maxima's quarrel with her mother-in-law.

It was now the hottest season of the year, when it was impossible to be very active, or much out of doors. During those days the feeling of despondence began again to weigh heavily on my heart. I pondered on Irala's words, and prayed continually, but the illumination he had prophesied came not. When I preached, my voice was like the buzzing of summer flies to the people : they came and sat or knelt on the floor of the church, and heard me with stolid unmoved countenances, then went forth again unchanged in heart. After the morning Mass I would return to my house, and, sitting alone in my room, pass the sultry hours, immersed in melancholy thoughts, having no inclination to work. At such times the image of Marta, in all the beauty of her girlhood, crowned with her shining golden hair, would rise before me, until the tears gathering in my eyes would trickle through my fingers. Then too I often recalled that terrible scene in the wood—the crouching figure in its sordid rags, the glaring furious eyes —again those piercing shrieks seemed to ring through me, and fill the dark mountain's forest with echoes, and I would start up half maddened with the sensations of horror renewed within me.

And one day, while sitting in my room, with these memories only for company, all at once a voice in my soul told me that the end was approaching, that the crisis was come, and that to whichever side I fell, there I should remain through all eternity. I rose up from my seat staring straight before me, like one who sees an assassin enter his apartment dagger in hand and who nerves himself for the coming struggle. Instantly all my doubts, my fears, my unshapen thoughts found expression, and with a million tongues shrieked out in my soul against my Redeemer. I called aloud on Him to save me, but He

came not ; and the spirits of darkness, enraged at my long
resistance, had violently seized on my soul, and were
dragging it down to perdition. I reached forth my hands
and took hold of the crucifix standing near me, and clung
to it as a drowning mariner does to a floating spar. " Cast
it down ! " cried out a hundred devils in my ear.
" Trample under foot this symbol of a slavery which has
darkened your life and made earth a hell ! He that died
on the Cross is powerless now ; miserably do they perish
who put their trust in Him ! Remember Marta Riquelme,
and save yourself from her fate while there is time."

My hands relaxed their hold on the cross, and falling
on the stones, I cried aloud to the Lord to slay me and
take my soul, for by death only could I escape from that
great crime my enemies were urging me to commit.

Scarcely had I pronounced these words before I felt that
the fiends had left me, like ravening wolves scared from
their quarry. I rose up and washed the blood from my
bruised forehead, and praised God ; for now there was a
great calm in my heart, and I knew that He who died to
save the world was with me, and that His grace had
enabled me to conquer and deliver my own soul from
perdition.

From that time I began to see the meaning of Irala's
words, that it was for me and not for him to find the
solution of the mysteries which had troubled me, and that
I had already come near to finding it. I also saw the
reason of that sullen resistance to religion in the minds of
the people of Yala ; of the temptations which had
assailed me—the strange tempests of anger and the

carnal passions, never experienced elsewhere, and which had blown upon my heart like hot blighting winds ; and even of all the events of Marta Riquelme's tragic life ; for all these things had been ordered with devilish cunning to drive my soul into rebellion. I no longer dwelt persistently on that isolated event of her transformation, for now the whole action of that tremendous warfare in which the powers of darkness are arrayed against the messengers of the Gospel began to unfold itself before me.

In thought I went back to the time, centuries ago, when as yet not one ray of heavenly light had fallen upon this continent ; when men bowed down in worship to gods, which they called in their several languages Pachacamac, Viracocho, and many others ; names which being translated mean, The All-powerful, Ruler of Men, The Strong Comer, Lord of the Dead, The Avenger. These were not mythical beings ; they were mighty spiritual entities, differing from each other in character, some taking delight in wars and destruction, while others regarded their human worshippers with tolerant and even kindly feelings. And because of this belief in powerful benevolent beings some learned Christian writers have held that the aborigines possessed a knowledge of the true God, albeit obscured by many false notions. This is a manifest error ; for if in the material world light and darkness cannot mingle, much less can the Supreme Ruler stoop to share His sovereignty with Belial and Moloch, or in this continent, with Tupa and Viracocho : but all these demons, great and small, and known by various names, were angels of darkness who had divided amongst themselves this new world and the nations dwelling in it. Nor need we be astonished at finding here resemblance to the true religion —majestic and graceful touches suggesting the Divine Artist; for Satan himself is clothed as an angel of light, and scruples not to borrow the things invented by the Divine Intelligence. These spirits possessed unlimited power and authority; their service was the one great business of all men's lives; individual character and natural feelings were crushed out by an implacable despotism, and no person dreamed of disobedience to their decrees, interpreted by their high priests; but all men were engaged in raising colossal temples, enriched with gold and precious stones, to their honour, and priests and virgins in tens of thousands conducted their worship with a pomp and magnificence surpassing those of ancient Egypt or Babylon. Nor can we doubt that these beings often made use of their power to suspend the order of nature, transforming men into birds and beasts, causing the trembling of the earth which ruins whole cities, and performing many other stupendous miracles to demonstrate their authority or satisfy their malignant natures. The time came when it pleased the Ruler of the world to overthrow this evil empire, using for that end the ancient, feeble instruments despised of men, the missionary priests, and chiefly those of the often persecuted Brotherhood founded by Loyola, whose zeal and holiness have always been an offence to the proud and carnal-minded. Country after country, tribe after tribe, the old gods were deprived of their kingdom, fighting always with all their weapons to keep back the tide of conquest. And at length, defeated at all points, and like an army fighting in defence of its territory, and gradually retiring before the invader to concentrate itself in some apparently inaccessible region and there stubbornly resist to the end ; so have all the old gods and demons retired into this secluded country, where, if they cannot keep out the seeds of truth they have at least succeeded in rendering the soil it falls upon barren as stone. Nor does it seem altogether strange that these once potent beings should be satisfied to remain in comparative obscurity and inaction when the entire globe is open to them, offering fields worthy of their evil ambition. For great as their power and intelligence must be they are, nevertheless, infinite beings, possessing, like man, individual characteristics, capabilities and limitations ; and after reigning where they have lost a continent, they may possibly be unfit or unwilling to serve elsewhere. For we know that even in the strong places of Christianity there are spirits enough for the evil work of leading men astray ; whole nations are given up to damnable heresies, and all religion is trodden under foot by many whose portion will be where the worm dieth not and the fire is not quenched.

From the moment of my last struggle, when this revelation began to dawn upon my mind, I have been safe from their persecutions. No angry passions, no sinful notions, no doubts and despondence disturb the peace of my soul. I was filled with fresh zeal, and in the pulpit felt that it was not my voice, but the voice of some mighty spirit speaking with my lips and preaching to the people with an eloquence of which I was not capable. So far, however, it has been powerless to win their souls. The old gods, although no longer worshipped openly, are their gods still, and could a new Tupac Amaru arise to pluck down the symbols of Christianity, and proclaim once more the Empire of the Sun, men would everywhere bow down to worship his rising beams and joyfully rebuild temples to the Lightning and the Rainbow.

Although the lost spirits cannot harm they are always near me, watching all my movements, ever striving to frustrate my designs. Nor am I unmindful of their presence. Even here, sitting in my study and looking out on the mountains, rising like stupendous stairs towards heaven and losing their summits in the gathering clouds, I seem to discern the awful shadowy form of Pachacamac, supreme among the old gods. Though his temples are in ruins, where the Pharaohs of the Andes and their millions of slaves worshipped him for a thousand years, he is awful still in his majesty and wrath that plays like lightning on his furrowed brows, kindling his stern countenance, and the beard which rolls downward like an immense white cloud to his knees. Around him gather other tremendous forms in their cloudy vestments—The Strong-Comer, the Lord of the Dead, The Avenger, The Ruler of Men, and many others whose names were once mighty throughout the continent. They have met to take counsel together; I hear their voices in the thunder hoarsely rolling from the hills, and in the wind stirring the forest before the coming tempest. Their faces are towards me, they are pointing to me with their cloudy hands, they are speaking of me— even of me, an old, feeble, worn-out man ! But I do not quail before them ; my soul is firm though my flesh is weak ; though my knees tremble while I gaze, I dare look forward even to win another victory over them before I depart.

Day and night I pray for that soul still wandering lost in the great wilderness ; and no voice rebukes my hope or tells me that my prayer is unlawful. I strain my eyes gazing out towards the forest ; but I know not whether Marta Riquelme will return to me with the tidings of her salvation in a dream of the night, or clothed in the garments of the flesh, in the full light of day. For her salvation I wait, and when I have seen it I shall be ready to depart ; for as the traveller, whose lips are baked with hot winds, and who thirsts for a cooling draught and swallows sand, strains his eyeballs to see the end of his journey in some great desert, so do I look forward to the goal of this life, when I shall go to Thee, O my Master, and be at rest !